# DIWALI
## A Festival of Lights

By Anita Yasuda
Illustrated by Darshika Varma

A GOLDEN BOOK • NEW YORK

Text copyright © 2024 by Anita Yasuda
Cover and interior illustrations copyright © 2024 by Darshika Varma
All rights reserved. Published in the United States by Golden Books, an imprint of Random House
Children's Books, a division of Penguin Random House LLC, 1745 Broadway, New York, NY 10019.
Golden Books, A Golden Book, A Little Golden Book, the G colophon, and the distinctive gold spine
are registered trademarks of Penguin Random House LLC.
rhcbooks.com
Educators and librarians, for a variety of teaching tools, visit us at RHTeachersLibrarians.com
Library of Congress Control Number: 2023930115
ISBN 978-0-593-70387-8 (trade) — ISBN 978-0-593-70388-5 (ebook)
Printed in the United States of America
10 9 8 7 6 5 4 3 2

Tonight, family and friends will fill our home with joy. Diwali, the Festival of Lights, is nearly here. On a dark night, thousands of bright lights and rows of lamps will shimmer.

Diwali takes place every year in October or November and is celebrated by Hindus, Sikhs, Jains, and some Buddhists.

Why do we celebrate Diwali? For over two thousand years, people have told different stories of how good wins over evil. One Hindu tale is about Rama. He defeated the demon king and found his way home thanks to all the lights people had set out for him to follow.

Diwali began in India. Now it has spread across the world. Leicester, a city in England, hosts the largest celebration in the United Kingdom. People can ride a Ferris wheel called the Diwali Wheel of Light.

In Suriname—a country in South America—the festival is called Deepavali. There are parades with music and dancing.

The festival is called Tihar in Nepal, South Asia. On the second day of Tihar, dogs are honored. Crows, cows, and oxen are celebrated on other days.

Diwali marks the start of the Hindu New Year. Celebrations last up to five days. We buy new clothes for the holiday and wear something gold and silver for good luck.

Some shops sell statues of Lakshmi—the goddess of wealth, love, and joy—and Ganesha—the god with the head of an elephant—to be worshipped. There are stalls with puffed rice snacks and sugary sweets shaped like animals.

We clean our house from top to bottom.

We believe the goddess Lakshmi enters each home to bless it, so we leave a window open for her. Will Lakshmi visit us tonight?

We decorate our home for our Diwali party. We make a rangoli pattern by the entrance. We draw loops and leaves or flowers with colored chalk or sand. The rangoli symbolizes happiness and welcomes guests to come inside.

We hang a string of flowers called a toran over the front door. Our toran has golden marigolds with mango leaves.

We make sweets as offerings for the gods during
our prayers called puja. We have creamy halwa topped
with raisins and yellow laddoos. The kheer looks like
pudding and tastes of cardamom. We light incense in
our puja room and present our offerings on a large
plate called a thali. Our thali has rice grains, dry fruits,
and kumkum powder.

Later, we wear our new clothes and visit the temple. All our friends are here!

Back home, we hang fairy lights and arrange candles on fancy trays. Tiny clay lamps called diyas look like twinkling raindrops. We line our walkway with lights, too. They glow warm and soft.

We paint designs called mehndi on our hands.
Our hands look like a garden of flowers.

Our guests are here! We bite into crunchy pakoras and golden samosas. We eat yummy pistachio barfi and fried dough called gulab jamun.

We exchange mithai gift boxes of fruits, nuts, and sweets with friends and talk to family far away.

In the evening we have glow sticks in blues, greens, and pinks. We wave sparklers in the air. There are balloons filled with colorful paper. *Pop!*

We watch fireworks. *Whizz! Boom!* And we release
paper lanterns into the sky. Their light reminds us that
good wins over evil.

# A Glossary of Words and Phrases

**barfi** (*baar-fee*): creamy, fudgelike sweet

**cardamom** (*kaar-duh-muhm*): whole or ground seeds of an herb used as a spice

**Diwali** (*dih-wah-lee*): Festival of Lights; also called Deepavali

**diya** (*dee-uh*): oil lamp made of clay

**Ganesha** (*guh-nay-shuh*): Hindu god of luck, success, and fortune

**gulab jamun** (*goo-laab ja-muhn*): fried dough with sticky syrup

**halwa** (*hal-wuh*): pudding-like sweet

**kheer** (*keer*): rice pudding

**kumkum** (*come-come*): red powder often used to make a dot on the forehead

**laddoo** (*luh-doo*): ball-shaped sweet

**Lakshmi** (*luhksh-mee*): Hindu goddess of luck, joy, and fortune

**mehndi** (*men-dee*): design made on the skin with henna

**mithai** (*mu-tai*): Indian sweets, sometimes coated with nuts and gold foil

**pakora** (*pe-ko-ra*): fritter usually made with vegetables

**puja** (*poo-jah*): prayer

**Rama** (*rah-muh*): hero in an ancient Hindu poem and form of the Hindu god Vishnu

**rangoli** (*ran-goh-lee*): design created on the floor with colorful sand, chalk, or flower petals

**samosa** (*sa-mo-sa*): triangular pastry often stuffed with potato

**Shubh Diwali!** (*shope dih-wah-lee*): Happy Diwali!

**thali** (*taa-lee*): large platter

**toran** (*tor-n*): decorative hanging, traditionally made of marigolds and mango leaves